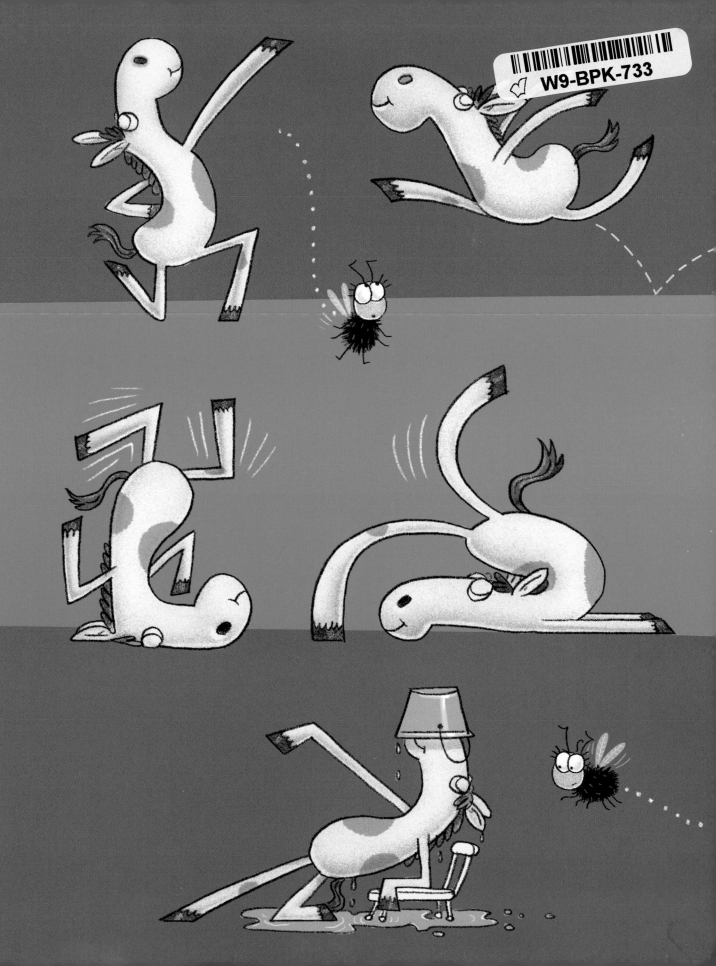

I Like to Read® books, created by award-winning
picture book artists as well as talented newcomers,
instill confidence and the joy of reading in new readers.

We want to hear every new reader say, "I like to read!"

Visit our website for flash cards, activities, and more about the series:
www.holidayhouse.com/ILiketoRead
#ILTR
This book has been tested by an educational expert
and determined to be a guided reading level E.

HORSE & BUGGY

DANCE, DANCE, DANCE!

Ethan Long

I Like to Read®

HOLIDAY HOUSE • NEW YORK

What are you doing?

I am dancing.

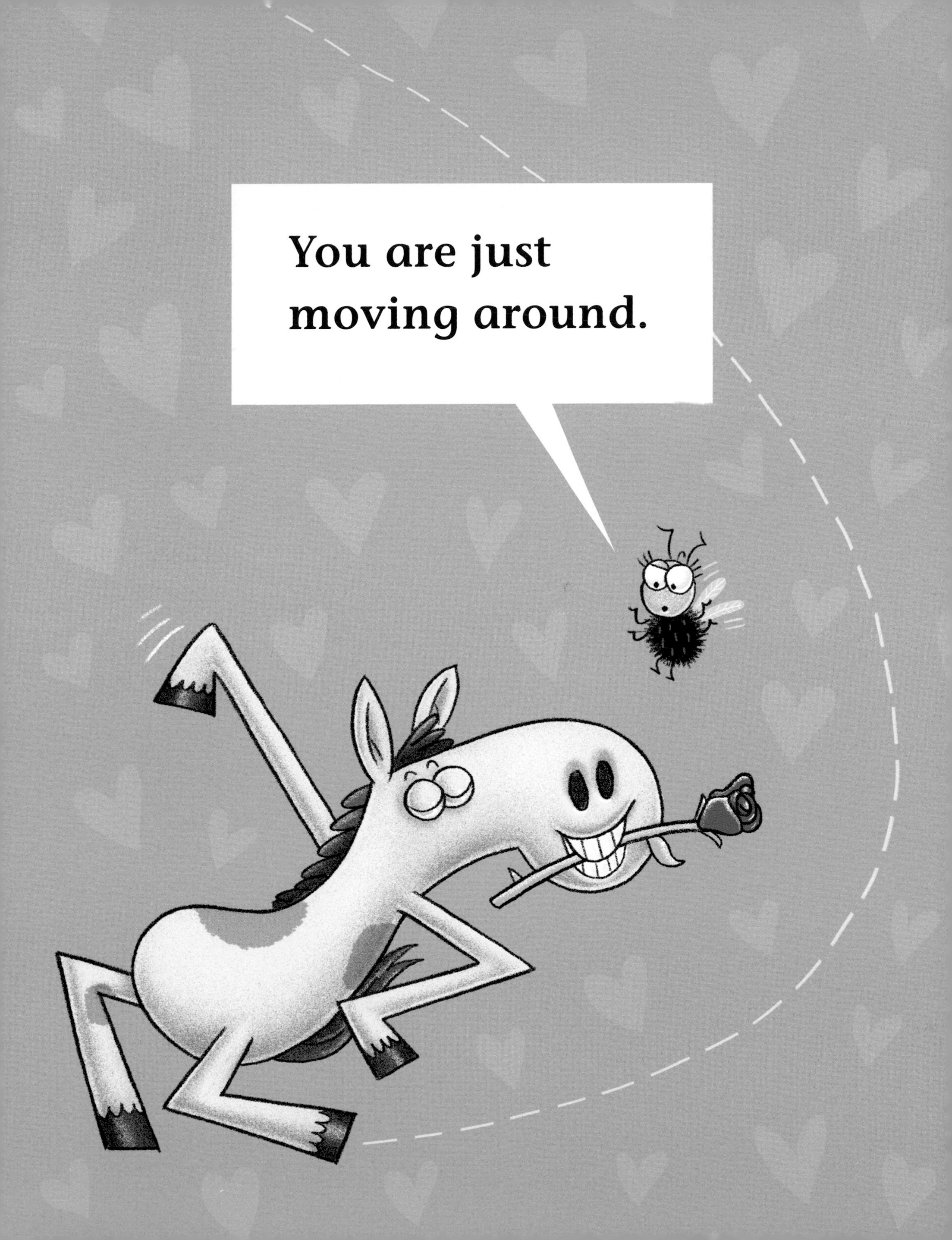
You are just moving around.

Come on!
Dance with me.

Not now.

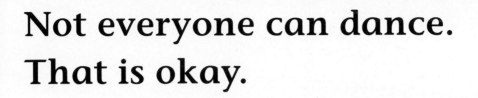

Not everyone can dance.
That is okay.

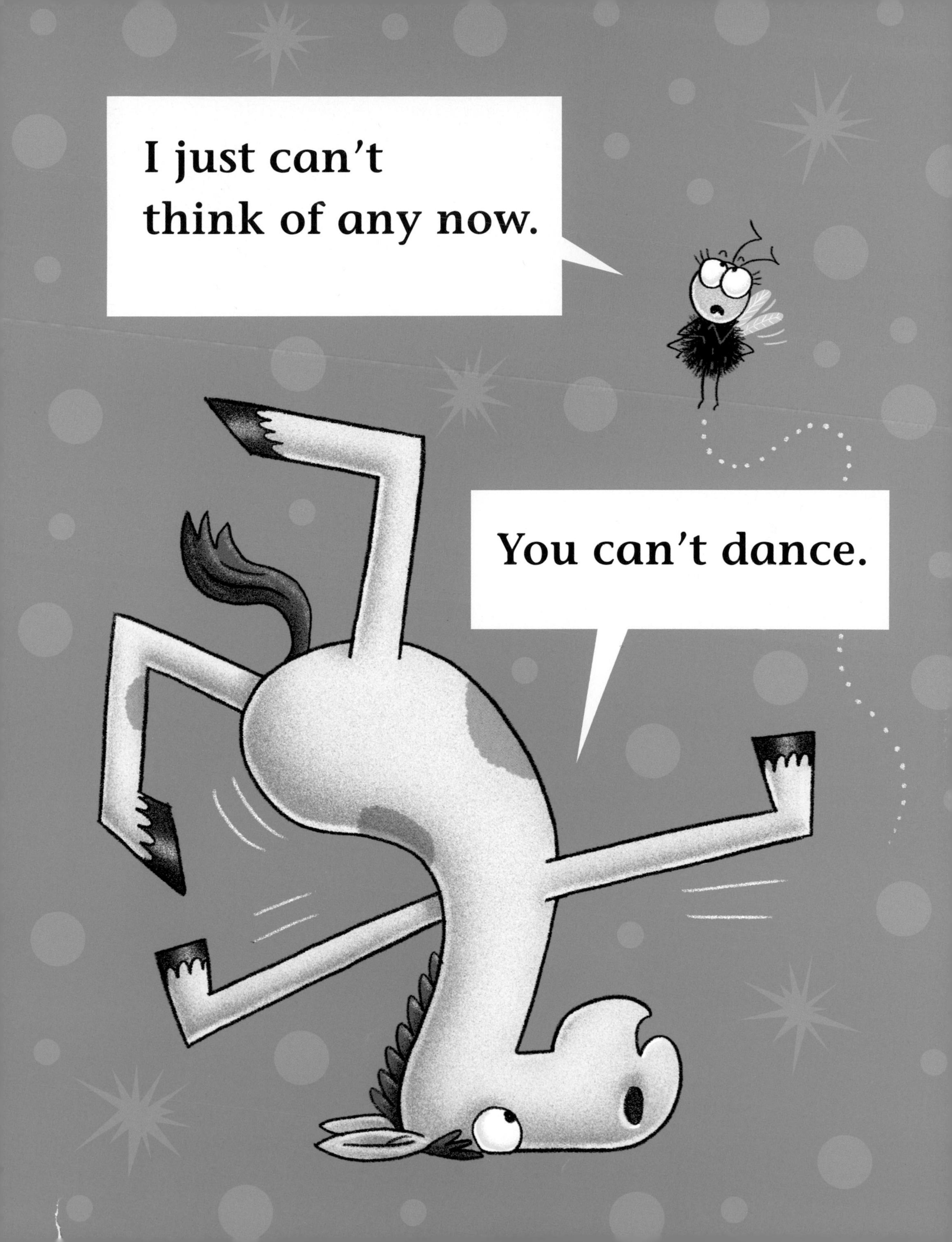
I just can't
think of any now.
You can't dance.

There. I danced.
Are you happy now?

Horse?

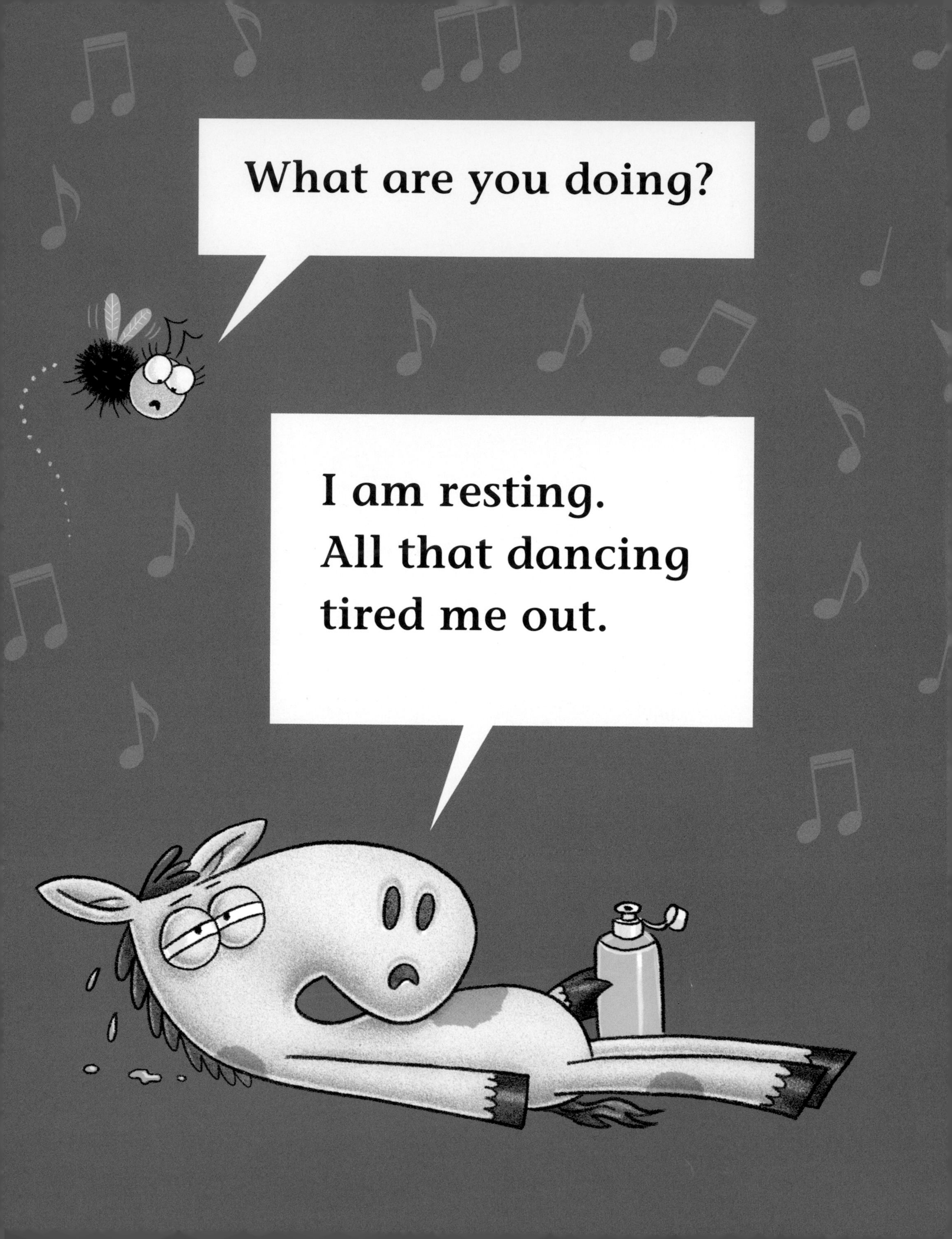
What are you doing?
I am resting. All that dancing tired me out.

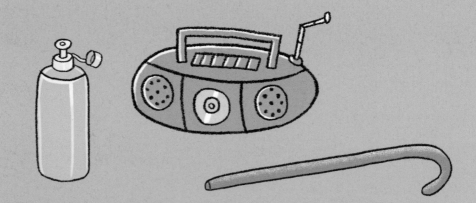

I LIKE TO READ is a registered trademark of Holiday House Publishing, Inc.

Copyright © 2018 by Ethan Long

HOLIDAY HOUSE is registered in the U.S. Patent and Trademark Office.

Printed and Bound in December 2018 at Tien Wah Press, Johor Bahru, Johor, Malaysia.

The artwork was created digitally.

www.holidayhouse.com

First Edition

3 5 7 9 10 8 6 4

Library of Congress Cataloging-in-Publication Data is available.

ISBN 978-0-8234-3859-4 (hardcover)

ISBN 978-0-8234-3968-3 (paperback)